Dev and Ollie

Colour Carnival

SHWETA AGGARW

Dev and Ollie

Colour Carnival

First published by Curious Minds Press Ltd in 2016
ISBN-13: 978-0-993-2328-1-7
ISBN-10: 0993232817

Edited by Graham Whitlock
Title Suggested by Rishi Mistry

www.devandollie.com

To our wonderful
world of colours!

INTRODUCING...

Dev

Cheeky, clumsy
and very curious.
A HUGE football fan!

Ollie

Dev's magical bedtime owl.
Always eager to take off
on adventures.

Mum

Wishes Dev would
enjoy messy play.

The girl

Waits eagerly for the
festival of colours
every year!

The other children

Look mean at first
but are really
just playful.

They continued to wrestle mid-air, **so hard** that Ollie's glasses fell off.

Still battling, Dev slipped off and clung onto Ollie's neck.

"We're falling!" spluttered Ollie.

They finally landed with a **bump**...but in the wrong city!

"Now look what you've done! We were meant to be going to Delhi but we've ended up in Agra," said Ollie.

"Never mind, Holi is celebrated across India."

"So the **whole** country gets coloured!" exclaimed Dev.

"Well, not me."

"But it's fun. Look," said Ollie.

From behind the tree, Dev saw
people covered in different colours.

Dancing, singing and playing,
everyone was enjoying themselves.

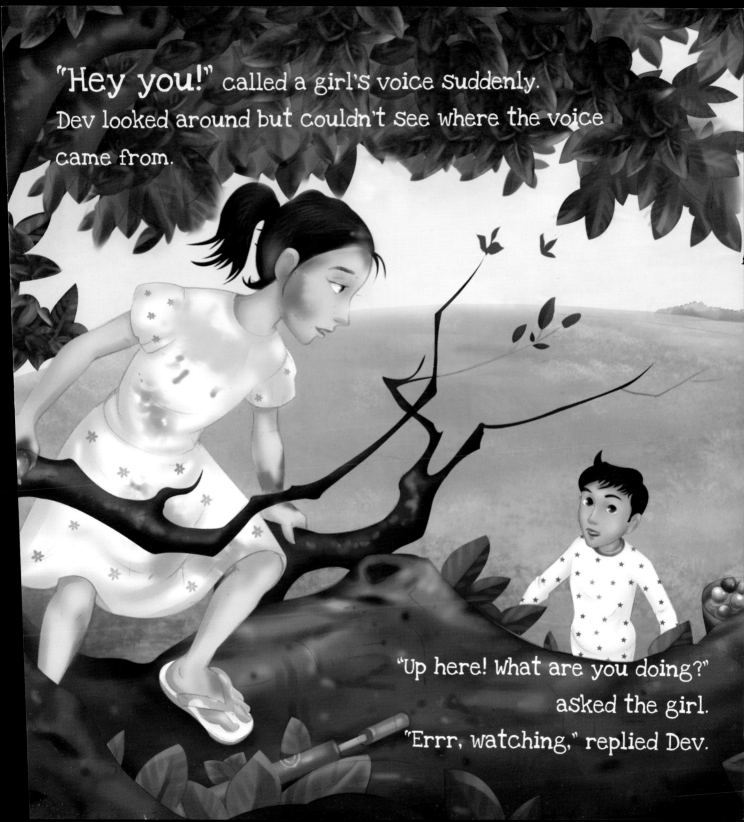

"Hey you!" called a girl's voice suddenly. Dev looked around but couldn't see where the voice came from.

"Up here! What are you doing?" asked the girl.

"Errr, watching," replied Dev.

The girl jumped down and said, "watching is not allowed.

Help me, I'm in the middle of a water balloon fight with those kids."

Before Dev could explain that he didn't like getting dirty, a water balloon hit him. And it was filled with paint!

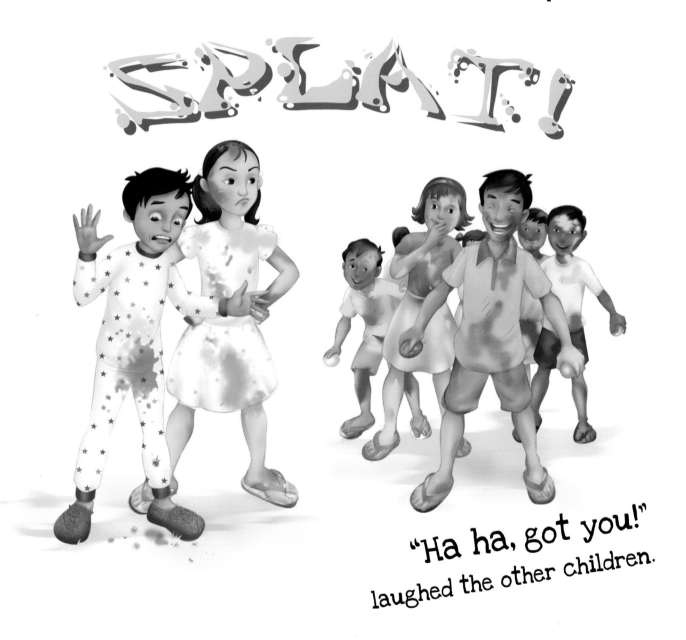

SPLAT!

"Ha ha, got you!" laughed the other children.

"Don't mind them. Everything is fair when playing Holi," said the girl.

But Dev was furious! He picked up a water balloon and **flung** it across.

"That was fun," thought Dev smiling for the first time.

The other children sprayed
Dev and the girl with
their water pistols.

"I left mine up in the tree," said the girl.

"I'll get it for you," said Dev. He reached the water pistol easily but got stuck on the way down.

"Hold **tight!!**" said the girl.

The children slowly pushed a huge barrel of water beneath Dev.

"Ok, jump now," said the girl.

"But that water is murky!" yelled Dev.

"You're **already** so mucky," chuckled Ollie.

Dev FINALLY jumped.

Stepping out of the barrel,
he slipped over, ending
up covered in ashes.

"I can't get any dirtier!" laughed Dev at last.
"Where did these ashes come from?"

"The ashes are from the Holika
bonfire last night. That's how
the festival of Holi begins,"
said the girl.

"Years ago, people used to play with ashes from the bonfire to
celebrate Holi. Aren't colours more fun? Let's go now

Together they ran into the crowd.

"Thank goodness!!" thought Ollie. "Dev's finally joining in."

When it came time to go home, Ollie tugged on a boy's shoulder.

"Hey! Let go!" said the boy.

"Uh-oh!" said Ollie. "Sorry, I mistook you for my friend Dev."

Luckily, Ollie
soon found Dev.

"You're so coloured I didn't
even recognise you!"
laughed Ollie.

Dev gave Ollie a tight
squeeze and together they
left Agra to head back home.

"Look below, Dev. It's the Taj Mahal, one of the greatest **wonders of the world,**" said Ollie gliding past.

'It's sooo white! Let's add some colour to it," chuckled Dev.

"OH NO! This is beautiful as it is, don't you think?" asked Ollie.

In the morning when Mum entered Dev's room, She found him covered in paint!

"What have you done to your pyjamas?" cried Mum.

Dev pulled out a painting. **Mum gasped.**

Then to Dev's surprise, she gave him a big hug!

'I'm **So** happy to finally see you enjoying painting!!" said Mum.

"Now let's give you a good scrub, you're quite dirty."

"Not dirty Mum, colourful," smiled Dev.

"Ready for the painting class now?"
whispered Ollie.

"Can't wait!"
beamed Dev.

"And Happy Holi, Ollie!"